River Eyes

Joan Lingard was born in Edinburgh
but grew up in Belfast. She has always
been an avid reader and started
writing when she was very young.
She has now published more than
thirty books for children.

She is married with three children and
five grandchildren, and now lives in
Edinburgh, Scotland.

Other story books by Joan Lingard:

TOM AND THE TREE HOUSE

THE EGG THIEVES

Other Hodder story books you may enjoy:

THE FAIRY COW

Ann Turnbull

SECRET FRIENDS

Elizabeth Laird

THE DRAGON'S CHILD

Jenny Nimmo

MILLY

Pippa Goodhart

River Eyes

JOAN LINGARD

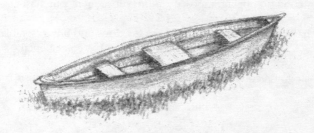

illustrated by Paul Howard

Hodder
Children's
Books

a division of Hodder Headline

For Rosa, Aedan, Shona and Amy

Chapter One

'I'd rather you didn't,' said Grandma.

'Didn't what?' asked Claire, coming into the kitchen.

'Well, we're going,' said Grandpa, not giving her an answer. He was looking at Grandma.

'Going where?' asked Claire.

'Grandpa and I are going on a canoeing trip down the river tomorrow and camping out overnight,' said Jamie. He didn't add, 'So there!'

but he might as well have done, he sounded so pleased with himself.

'Can I come?' asked Claire.

'Certainly not!' said Grandma. 'I've enough to worry about without you going too.' She was standing at the sink washing her paint-brushes. She swirled the water noisily around, splashing some on her front.

'Why shouldn't I go?' demanded Claire. 'Why should *he* – she pointed at her brother who was smirking – 'go and not me? It's not fair!'

'I'm older than you,' said Jamie. 'Bigger and stronger. You have to be strong for a long canoe trip.'

'*I'm* strong!' Claire made a fist and strengthened the muscle in her upper arm. Not much of a bulge showed so she let the arm drop. 'That's not the real reason, is it?' She turned to her grandfather. 'It's because I'm a girl and he's a boy.'

'Of course it's not! I wouldn't dare treat you differently because you're a girl. Your grandmother would skin me alive if I did!' He smiled across at his wife. 'Wouldn't you, dear?'

She gave him a look and went on with her paint-brush washing. She had a smudge of green paint on her cheek. She often had smudges on her cheek.

'Grandma's worried in case the canoe tips over and we drown,' said Jamie. He wasn't worried. Far from it. He couldn't wait to go!

'Don't even say such things!' said Grandma. She laid the brushes out on the draining-board in a row to dry.

'I'm a good swimmer,' said Claire. 'I beat you last week, didn't I, Jamie?' Now she smirked at her brother. They had raced one another in their local swimming pool and she had won 50p in a bet.

'I think you're right, Claire,' put in Grandpa. 'You are old enough now to come with us.'

'Fantastic!' Claire let out a cheer.

Jamie was not looking so pleased. Nor was Grandma.

'For your information, Margaret,' said Grandpa to his wife, 'we do not intend to fall in the river.' In the meantime he had been laying out his fishing tackle.

'I shan't sleep a wink if you go,' declared Grandma.

'You'll just have to stay awake then, won't you?'

She snorted. 'Why not go canoeing but come back to sleep? I really don't like the idea of you camping on the riverbank.'

What could happen to us?' asked Jamie.

'We could catch pneumonia,' said Grandpa. 'Or a bear might eat us.' He liked to tease his wife. And she liked to tease him in return,

'There could be poachers about,'

she said, not teasing him now. She
sounded serious.

'Poachers!' he scoffed. 'I've fished
that river for the last twenty years and
I've never clapped eyes on a poacher.'

'But you've never stayed overnight,'
said Grandma.

'What do poachers do?' asked Claire.

'They steal salmon,' said Grandma.

'*Salmon?*' To Claire that seemed a funny thing to steal. 'Why would they want to steal salmon?'

'Because they sell for a lot of money, stupid!' said her brother.

'Stupid yourself!' She tossed her head at him and turned back to her grandfather. 'Can't anyone go fishing where they like?'

'Oh no! You have to pay whoever owns the fishing rights. Fish are getting scarcer and scarcer. If people were allowed to take what they wanted there'd soon be none left.'

'Poaching is big business in Scotland, isn't it, Duncan?' said Grandma.

Her husband nodded. 'They steal fish and sell it into markets in Glasgow and Edinburgh. London, too.'

'Don't they work in gangs?' said Grandma.

'Gangs?' said Jamie, his eyes widening. 'They might have guns.'

'It is extremely unlikely that there are any armed poachers on our river,' said Grandpa. 'I've never heard the slightest whisper of any.'

The phone rang then, stopping any further discussion. Claire reached it first.

'Oh, hi, Mum!' she said. 'Yes, we're having a lovely holiday. I went out painting with Grandma this morning. I did a picture of a Highland cow. One of those nice goldeny ones with the shaggy hair over their eyes.'

'You could have fooled me,' said Jamie. 'I thought it was meant to be a dinosaur.'

Claire stuck her tongue out at him.

'Now, Jamie!' said Grandma. 'It was *very* good. I'm going to put it on the wall.'

The walls were covered with paintings done by her as well as other artists. She sold her pictures at exhibitions.

'And Grandpa's going to take Jamie and me canoeing on the river,' Claire went on. 'We're going to camp out overnight.'

She listened to her mother for a moment and then held out the receiver to her grandfather. 'Grandpa, Mum wants a word.'

'I bet she does,' said Grandma.

Grandpa took the phone. 'Now don't you worry your head, Jane. You'll end up as bad as your mother!'

'Some of us are more responsible than others,' said his wife.

'The children will be in no danger, dear, I assure you,' continued Grandpa on the telephone. 'They will have life jackets on every single moment they're in the canoe. And you know I was an expert canoer in my youth.'

'You're not in your youth now,' muttered Grandma.

He covered the receiver with his hand. 'I'm not so old, either.'

Claire had collapsed into the rocking chair and was rocking herself to and fro. Jamie was scowling – he liked going off with Grandpa on his own.

'So don't worry, Jane,' said Grandpa. 'The canoe is completely river-worthy. And your mother will see to it that we all have plenty of warm clothes with us and enough food to feed a regiment.

So you can sleep soundly. The children will be perfectly safe in my hands.'

'They'd better be,' said Grandma as he put down the phone.

Chapter Two

They spent the rest of the afternoon getting ready for their trip. Grandma made bread and Jamie and Claire managed to bake a banana cake between them without falling out. Grandma warned them beforehand.

'You've got to learn to co-operate.'

'Especially if you're coming out with me in the canoe,' said Grandpa. 'No bickering allowed.'

He was checking out the tent,

making sure everything was intact and that all the pegs were there. One was missing and he had to go back up to the loft to look for it.

'We'll need the camping stove and the picnic plates and cutlery,' he said, when he came back down. 'They're all in the shed.'

The children fetched them and set them out on the kitchen table.

'What will we have for supper when we camp?' asked Claire.

'Trout and mushrooms,' said Grandpa. 'I'll take care of the trout and you two can pick the mushrooms.'

The woods were full of the little yellow mushrooms called chanterelles. It was turning out to be a good year for them. Sometimes there were a lot; at other times, not. It depended on how much rain there'd been.

Until recently the weather had been wet. Grandpa had been waiting for a dry spell so that they could make their river trip.

The children were always careful when they picked mushrooms. Their grandfather had trained them to recognise the ones that were safe to eat. Some were poisonous. Grandpa always said not to touch any that they weren't certain about.

'I'll put in a tin of beans and some eggs, just in case,' said Grandma.

'In case of what?' asked Grandpa.

'Just in case you don't catch any trout. Well, it's possible, isn't it?' Grandma smiled sweetly.

'Grandpa always gets something,' said Jamie. 'Well, nearly always.' He liked to fish himself but Claire didn't. Thank goodness for that!

When anything exciting happened she jumped about like a grasshopper. If he got a fish hooked she'd be bound to scare it away.

'Thank you, Jamie,' said Grandpa. To his wife he added, 'It's just as well somebody's got faith in me!'

She just gave him another of her smiles.

By the time she had finished with the food she had two huge bagfuls set out for them to take.

'We're not going for a week!' protested Grandpa.

'I wouldn't mind if we were,' said Jamie.

'Perhaps next year,' said Grandpa.

'Over my dead body!' said Grandma. 'I don't mind not sleeping for one night but for a week? No way!'

Claire found it difficult to get to sleep that night. She pulled the curtain aside to watch the sky darkening. It was still light until late, gone ten, even though it was now the month of August. That was because they were so far north.

There was a full moon, too. It hung up there above the ridge of the hills, pale white against the indigo blue of the sky. Gradually as the sky darkened the moon deepened to a real yellow.

Claire fell asleep and dreamed she was in a boat rocking to and fro.

Jamie had fallen asleep quickly but he woke early to the morning chatter of the birds. He raised himself on one elbow. The house itself was quiet. He dressed and let himself out.

The grass was soft with dew. He slipped out of the gate and went down through the small birch wood to the river.

A deer crossed the path in front of him leaping swiftly and lightly away into the trees. There were a great many deer about – too many, his grandfather said. They were roe deer, sandy-brown coloured, smaller than red deer. But they had big appetites! They did a lot of damage. They ate young tree shoots in the woods and the herbs and flowers in Grandma's garden. Jamie, though, loved the way the deer moved. He wished he could run and jump as gracefully as they did. As if it was no bother at all.

A light grey mist was hovering over the water but that would lift as the sun came up. The day promised to be fine. A good day for canoeing. His grandfather had been promising him this trip for the last two years.

He heard something move further along the bank. This time it was not a deer. Deer made little if any noise. No more than a whisper. Jamie shrank back into the shelter of the trees. There was a man further along there on the bank. Jamie could just make out his shape through the branches.

His heart beat faster. What if it was a poacher? Jamie craned his neck to get a better view and lost his footing. He stepped on a fallen branch.

The noise sounded like an explosion in his ears.

'Who's there?' called the man.

Jamie wondered whether to make a run for it. The man was coming towards him. He was wearing chest-high waders and a green fisherman's jacket and he was carrying a fishing rod. Jamie recognised him then and felt an idiot for suspecting him of being a poacher. It was Rory, the local gamekeeper.

'Is that you, young Jamie?' said Rory. 'I hear your Grandpa's taking you down the river today. He was on the phone last night asking if it'd be all right for you to camp.'

'Rory, have you ever seen any poachers on the river?'

'The odd one. Matter of fact – ' He stopped.

Jamie looked at him.

'We *have* heard the odd rumour

recently,' Rory went on. 'But it's probably only a rumour so I wouldn't worry your head over it. I'm sure it's OK.'

Nor would Jamie worry his grandfather's head over it. If he did, Grandpa – or Grandma – might decide against their river trip.

'I'll need to be going,' he said. He'd better get back before they missed him!

The mist on the water was thinning, the sky was turning rosy.

'Enjoy your river trip!' said Rory.

'I will!' said Jamie.

His grandmother was boiling the kettle as he came in.

'It's a nice morning,' he said.

'It is that,' she agreed. 'Now you see and keep your wits about you on that river today, Jamie. And keep an eye on that grandfather of yours!'

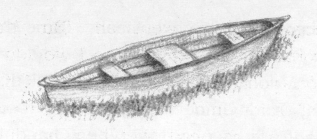

Chapter Three

Grandma came down to the river to see them off and help carry.

'The canoe won't sink, will it?' asked Claire as she watched it being loaded up.

What a lot of stuff they seemed to be taking! There was the tent, which luckily was light-weight, and their sleeping bags and spare clothes which they would need if they got wet. The camping stove and billy-cans and plates went in next. Finally, came the two sacks of food.

'I don't think we can take all that lot,' said Grandpa, eyeing the food. 'Half will have to do.' When Grandma started to protest he added, 'You don't *want* us to sink, do you?'

'You're always telling me what a stout canoe it is,' she responded. 'Built to shoot the rapids in the Canadian Rockies.'

'And so it would, given the chance,' he agreed cheerfully.

'Can we go to Canada sometime, Grandpa?' asked Claire.

'Not today.'

Grandma was busy halving the food, deciding what could be left behind. The children hopped around on the bank, getting more and more excited until Grandpa had to tell them to calm down.

'You'll fall into the river if you're not careful!' he warned. 'Now let me see that your jackets are properly fastened.'

He made them stand still while he checked. They had worn life jackets before. Last summer they'd gone on a course at a water sports centre to learn the basics of canoeing.

'Remember,' he told them, 'if the boat *should* tip – which we don't expect it to do – you must stay with it and hang on. And don't ever stand up in it!'

They nodded. Then he pushed the canoe into the water and held it against the bank. Grandma crouched down and helped to hold it steady.

'Now, Jamie, you first!' said Grandpa. 'You go into the bow.'

Jamie took his seat at the front of

the boat and Grandpa passed him a paddle.

'Right, Claire, you're in the middle.'

She climbed in. 'I wish I could have a paddle.'

'We'll give you a go later,' promised Grandpa. 'But it's easier just to have two paddling.'

'See you tomorrow!' He kissed Grandma. 'Now, Margaret, please don't spend the next twenty-four hours worrying! We are going to be perfectly all right.'

'I shall put you right out of my mind,' said Grandma, but they didn't believe that.

'What are you going to do with yourself?'

'I thought I'd take the car and spend the day sketching.'

'You won't try to follow us down the river, will you?' said Grandpa suspiciously.

'How could I do that? Follow you down the river in a car! Off you go and enjoy yourselves! See you tomorrow.' They had arranged to meet up at midday, further downstream.

Grandpa took his place in the back of the canoe and pushed it out from the bank.

'Ready then, Jamie? Try to keep in time with me. In, out, in, out, that's it. Good lad! You've got the rhythm going nicely.'

Their paddles dipped smoothly in and out of the water. They were moving well and gradually picking up speed. Grandma stood watching from the bank until they reached a bend in the river overhung with trees. And then she was out of sight.

'Easy does it, Jamie,' said Grandpa. 'You're doing splendidly, though.'

Jamie was puffing a little and red in the face. Claire trailed her hand in the water. She loved the golden-brown colour that came from the peat on the river-bed.

After an hour Grandpa decided they needed a rest. Jamie was glad of one though he didn't say so. Claire would demand to take his place if he did! She'd soon tire, though, for her arms really were not as strong as his. Paddling was good fun but hard work.

They might as well have an early lunch, Grandpa decided. They ate the cheese and salad sandwiches Grandma had made with her fresh brown bread and drank orange juice. While they ate they watched the birds on the river.

They saw a number of ducks and two herons in flight.

The sun was warm on their faces and the few clouds overhead were puffy and white.

What a perfect day it was for being on the river!

Rested, they set off again, passing fields where sheep and sometimes horses grazed. And now came a house whose garden bordered the water's edge, with only a dry stone dyke separating it. Two small boys playing with a red and white spotted ball waved to them and Claire waved back. They saw no one else.

At six, they berthed for the evening at a spot that Grandpa knew well. He often fished here. The beat belonged to his friend Hector. Rory the gamekeeper worked for Hector.

They pulled the canoe up out of the water and laid it upside down on the grass.

'Just in case it should rain,' said Grandpa. 'We don't want it full of water.'

'The sky's clear,' said Jamie, looking up.

'Aye, but you can never tell. The weather can change in a twinkling up here.'

They decided to pitch the tent a little way back from the bank on the edge of a birch wood.

'The trees will give us a bit of shelter should a wind come up,' said Grandpa.

They unrolled their sleeping bags. Claire felt excited as she laid hers out.

'Now for supper!' said Grandpa. 'We have to catch our own food.' He liked the idea of being self-sufficient, as he called it. He was going to fish his favourite pool which was close by. Claire asked if she and Jamie could go and pick mushrooms.

'I'd rather you waited for me. You know I don't like you going off on your own.'

'But we'd just be right here,' objected Jamie.

'Please, Grandpa!' said Claire.

'We wouldn't go far, Grandpa,' promised Jamie. 'Honestly we wouldn't.'

'Oh, well, all right. But don't go very far into the wood, OK?'

'OK,' they agreed.

'We can shout if we need you,' said Claire. 'And we know where you'll be.'

Grandpa put on his waders and went down to the riverbank. The children took a plastic bag and headed into the wood.

Usually they went mushrooming with a wicker basket so that the mushroom spores could fall through the gaps in the weave. It was a bit like planting seeds in the ground so that you'd get a crop next year. But there hadn't been room in the canoe for something as knobbly and awkward as a basket.

They walked bent over, looking like half-shut knives. Their eyes raked the ground, seeking out little daubs of yellow.

'I see one!' shouted Claire and she pounced.

'No need to scream!' said Jamie.

She was rummaging in moss. She withdrew her hand. Cupped in the hollow of her palm was a fluted, canary yellow mushroom. A chanterelle.

Now that they had come upon one
they found another close by. They
often grew in clusters. Searching was
good fun – it was like a treasure hunt.
And at the end of it they would have a
pile of lovely things to eat!

When they had exhausted the first spot they moved a little further into the wood, keeping their eyes glued to the ground. Pickings were scarcer here. They had to search carefully. They didn't have much luck under the trees where it was dark. It was better in clearings where the sun had a chance to shine through. Chanterelles needed rain to swell them up but also sun to bring them out. And they liked birch trees.

'I see a whole lot more!' cried Claire and she went sprinting towards a rash of yellow. Grandma said she had sharp eyes.

She knelt down. This was a real find! There seemed to be hundreds. Well, maybe not hundreds, but definitely a lot. Claire began to pick. When she had a small mound of mushrooms at her feet she glanced round to tell Jamie to come and give her a hand. She couldn't see him.

'Jamie!' she called. She listened but heard only the high call of a bird.

They must have wandered away from each other without realising it. Jamie must be somewhere close by, though, and would catch up with her soon. She put as many mushrooms as she could get into her pocket. She hated leaving the rest but Jamie had the bag.

There was still no sign of her brother. She would have to go back and look for him. She had come into a little hollow where the trees were more thinly spaced. She turned around in a circle. There were paths running in every direction. Which one had she come by? They all looked the same.

For a moment she panicked and then she made herself calm down. Count to ten, her mum always said when you feel panicky. She counted now.

When she reached ten she took a deep breath and studied the paths again. She would have to choose one. She couldn't stand there for the rest of the evening waiting to be rescued. Jamie might have gone

in the opposite direction. She was bound to come out to the edge of the wood eventually, wasn't she? Then she could work her way round it until she found the river.

She did 'eeny-meeny-miney-mo' and chose a path. 'Jamie!' she called as she walked. Maybe he was lost as well. Was *she* lost? No! She couldn't be. Grandpa was not far away.

'Grandpa!' she shouted. Her voice echoed through the trees. She thought it sounded odd, not like her voice at all. *'Grandpa!'*

There was light up ahead. It must be the river! She began to run but then she saw that it was just another clearing, an opening in the wood, with a wide track leading away from it. The track was wide enough for a car.

There was a car in the clearing, and a man standing beside it.

Chapter Four

When Jamie looked up from his picking he couldn't see his sister. Scrambling to his feet, he called out to her. He called her name twice, cupping his hands round his mouth to throw his voice further.

'Claire! Where are you, Claire?'

Claire didn't answer. He felt cross with her. Grandpa had told her not to wander off. So which way had she gone?

He took one of the many paths, the widest one. He kept on calling. Her name went echoing through the trees in front of him. The path narrowed. The wood here was dense, dark and a bit scary. The trees were older, and some with tangled branches made weird shapes that made him think of witches' arms. Tracks ran in all directions, deer tracks mostly. Branches slapped against his face. He pushed them aside and stepped over other, fallen ones, and pressed on.

He stopped. He had to stop, for he knew he was getting nowhere. This was like being in a maze. He was encircled by trees, trees crowded close together, their branches interlocked. He could see nothing *but* trees. Now *he* was lost.

He had no idea which way back it would be to the river. He thought of his grandfather who would be getting frantic. He'd probably be vowing never to take them on a trip again.

Jamie stayed quite still and listened intently, with his ear cocked, as an animal might, trying to pick up sounds. A bird was calling to another high above. He thought, however, that he had heard something else. A different noise. But he might have been wrong. He listened again.

'Jamie!' It was Claire's voice, he was sure it was, faint but clear!

'I'm coming!' he yelled, plunging headlong down a track that seemed to lead in the direction of the sound.

She called again and this time her voice was louder. She kept calling and he kept following until he saw that the trees were beginning to thin ahead. As he reached the clearing a greyish-green vehicle drove off down a track on the other side, raising a fine spray of dust behind it. From that quick glimpse he thought it might have been a Land Rover.

Claire came rushing to meet him and flung herself into his arms.

'I was frightened, Jamie. I was lost, I didn't know which way to go!'

'You're all right now. I've found you, silly twit that you are, going off like that!'

'There was a man.'

'A man?' said Jamie, alarmed. 'Did he come near you?'

She shook her head.

'Did he speak to you?'

'He shouted at me.'

'*Shouted?*'

'Yes, he shouted, "Clear off!" in a horrible sort of voice.'

'Maybe he thought you were trespassing.'

'But it's not his wood, is it?'

No, it was not. It belonged to Hector and was looked after by Rory. So the man, whoever he was, had no right to tell Claire to 'clear off'. Why had he wanted her to clear off, anyway? She wasn't doing any harm. Jamie frowned but he thought they'd better not waste any more time worrying about that now. They had to find their way back to the river as fast as possible. Before Grandpa raised the alarm! The track that the car had taken should be the best bet, he reckoned. It ought to lead out of the wood.

'We won't mention the man to Grandpa, Claire,' said Jamie. 'He'll be worked up enough as it is.'

Jamie took his sister's hand and together they ran across the clearing. With his other hand he held on to the mushroom bag making sure they didn't spill. If they were to return without any supper that would be the last straw!

'I hope we don't meet that man,' said Claire.

'I expect he'll be miles away by this time.'

And, indeed, they saw no sign of him or of anyone else on the track. At the end of it they emerged onto a proper tarmacked road.

They looked right and then left. Which way should they go? There was no clue yet as to which direction the river lay. While they were standing there at the side of the road wondering, unable to decide, they heard a car coming. Claire shrank back but this car was red. A man was driving, with a woman in the front beside him. The car slowed as it approached and they saw that their grandfather was sitting in the back seat!

The back door opened and out he sprang. His face was bright red.

'Where have you two been?' he cried.

'In the wood,' said Claire.

'You've been away for two hours!'

'I'm sorry, Grandpa,' said Claire.

Jamie said nothing. He always kept his head down while a row was going on and waited for it to blow over. Claire was different. She could never keep quiet.

'Didn't I tell you not to go far?' demanded Grandpa.

'We didn't mean to,' said Claire.

'I was on my way to get help,' said Grandpa. 'These people here were kind enough to offer me a lift to the police station.'

Grandpa calmed down and thanked the couple for the lift. They asked if they could take them back to their campsite but Grandpa said thank you very much, but no, they would walk. The couple waved and the car drove away.

They set off for the river. The children walked one on either side of their grandfather, saying nothing while he gave them a long lecture on the dangers of getting lost in woods.

'It's a serious matter. People have sometimes been lost for a day or more. You were lucky. It's easy to keep wandering round and round and lose your sense of direction.'

Their tent was standing where they had left it, tucked inside the fringe of trees. No one had touched their things. Claire commented on that.

'Who would be around to touch them?' said Grandpa.

Claire opened her mouth again and then closed it as she saw her brother frowning at her. She had almost mentioned the man she had seen in the wood.

Chapter Five

Grandpa had caught one good-sized fish and three smaller ones. They were relieved he'd caught something. If he hadn't he might have been in an even worse mood! He was pleased, too, to see that their bag was half full of mushrooms. Jamie had lost only a few.

'So we have supper!' he said. They could see that Grandpa was already becoming less angry. He never stayed in a bad mood for long.

He had cleaned his
fish and now they must
clean their mushrooms.
They pulled off the
bits of grass and moss
that clung to them,
trimmed the stalks
and then wiped
the bulbs with
kitchen paper.
Grandpa said there was no need
to wash them – it would spoil them.

He lit the camping stove and put
some oil and a little butter into a pan.
When it began to sizzle, Claire tipped
in the mushrooms. They let them cook
until they were golden brown and
crispy. The pan was so small they
could cook only one thing at a time.
When the mushrooms were ready they
put them in a dish to keep warm

beside the stove and Grandpa laid his fish in the pan. The smells were making their mouths water. They realised they were starving!

'It's been a long time since lunch,' said Grandpa, looking stern for a moment.

'We're sorry, Grandpa,' said Claire.

They ate the mushrooms and fish with thick slices of Grandma's bread.

'Just as well your grandma didn't know that you got yourselves lost!' said Grandpa.

'We'll not tell her, will we?' said Claire.

'No, maybe not,' agreed Grandpa.

When they'd finished their first course they ate the banana cake – all of it – and some fruit, and by then they were full of food and sleepy. Claire couldn't stop yawning.

'You two get into your sleeping bags,' said Grandpa. 'It's been a long day. I'll clear up here.'

Claire was first to fall asleep that night. Jamie stayed awake, watching the light inside the tent fade. It was not going to be completely dark since the sky was clear and the moon would be up. He listened to the river, to the soft gentle sound that it made. An owl hooted. Then Grandpa moved outside and the tent flap opened. Jamie coughed.

'You still awake, lad?' asked Grandpa.

'Yes.'

'You've not got a cough, have you?'

'No. It's just a tickle.'

'It's a beautiful night out there.' Grandpa sighed. 'I love this river.'

So did Jamie. The thought of it

flowing smoothly and steadily between its grassy banks made him feel good. He would love to canoe down the river at night under the moon and the stars. But he knew his grandparents wouldn't go for that! Perhaps he would do it sometime when he was grown up. He turned over and slid into a deep, peaceful sleep.

In the early morning, his cough wakened him. It was just a tickle, he was sure, not a serious cough. But he could do with a drink of water. Grandpa and Claire were both sleeping soundly. Grandpa was lying on his back and snoring a little.

Jamie eased himself out of his sleeping bag and crept towards the entrance of the tent, stepping carefully over his sister. She stirred before settling again, muttering something he could not make out. She must be having a dream. Not a good one, from the sound of her muttering.

He untied the flap and crawled out. There had been a change in the weather, he felt it straight away. There was no longer a moon and the sky had clouded over. A grey dawn was breaking. Sky, land, river: all were grey. Raising his face, he felt soft spots of moisture.

Jamie's cough came on again reminding him of the reason he'd come out. He lifted the water bottle and tilting it back drank straight from the neck. The water was cool and refreshed his throat.

He decided to go down to the river, just for a moment. He couldn't resist it. That wouldn't count as straying, would it? He was still within hailing distance of the tent. He squatted on the bank. Even in this grey half-light he found the river magical.

Something moved further along the bank. It was a deer. There it went, crossing the river. Two swift bounds, scarcely disturbing the water, and it was on the other side. Now came another, as sure-footed as the first. And another! The three animals stopped on the opposite bank to graze. Jamie couldn't take his eyes off them.

One of the deer lifted its head and listened. The second one, alerted now, raised its head. The third followed suit. What could they hear? Something that he couldn't.

Suddenly, all three took flight and within seconds had disappeared.

Now Jamie himself could hear something further along the bank. He waited with his head raised, in the way that the deer had. No, he hadn't been mistaken. There was something – or somebody – there. He felt the back of his neck prickle.

Then he saw the black outlines of the two men. One stood on the opposite bank, the other on this side, not many metres away from Jamie. They were close to the salmon pool his grandfather had fished earlier. There was something dark also in the water, and it was moving. For a moment Jamie could not make out what it was. He thought it must be an animal, perhaps an otter, though it looked too big for that. As his eyes focused he recognised the head and shoulders of a man.

Chapter six

Jamie flattened himself in the heather. The man in the river appeared to be wearing a wet suit. His shoulders were black and shiny above the greyness of the water. He was pumping the water with his arms, agitating it. What was he doing? Suddenly Jamie realised. He was trying to send salmon into the pool! The other men were walking along the bank and they were pulling what looked like ropes.

Jamie felt the tickle in his throat again. He swallowed and told himself, 'Don't cough! Don't *dare* cough!' He held his breath. He thought he might be about to choke, or explode. The feeling gradually passed and he let out a long slow sigh. He ought to go and tell Grandpa but he was afraid to move.

The men were dragging something out of the river onto the bank. It was a net and obviously heavy. Jamie thought he saw a flash of silver. Fish? Were there fish in the net? The man in the wet suit was now clambering up out of the water himself and going to help the other two. They were all too busy to notice Jamie lurking in the undergrowth.

He began to crawl towards the tent, glad that the sound of the river would cover any slight scuffling noises that he himself made.

He reached the tent and put his head in.

'Grandpa,' he whispered, 'wake up! But don't speak out loud.'

'What's this?' Grandpa shot upright.

'Shh!' said Jamie. 'There are poachers on the river.'

'Poachers?' said Claire, opening her eyes. 'I was dreaming about poachers.'

Grandpa was out of his sleeping bag in a second and pulling on his trousers. Jamie hauled on his jeans. His T-shirt and shorts were soaking wet but he left them on. He quickly told his grandfather what he had seen.

'I'm coming too!' said Claire, unzipping her bag and getting dressed too.

'No, you're not!' said Grandpa.

'I don't want to stay here on my own,' she wailed. 'You can't leave me. I'd be scared.'

'Oh, all right! But you'll have to keep well back. We're all going to keep well back and quiet. Understand?'

Grandpa put his binoculars round his neck and led the way out of the tent and down to the river. They crept like animals on all fours. When they reached the bank they lay flat in the heather. It was starting to rain.

Grandpa raised his binoculars to his eyes. 'Difficult to see anything with this rain,' he muttered. He wiped the glass. 'I see them now. They've got their haul all right!' He wiped the glass again. 'They're wrapping up the fish and putting them in sacks. They're about to leave. They're taking the track that goes up to the road.'

'We could follow,' said Jamie.

'We couldn't stop them getting away.'

'But we might get their car number and then we could tell the police.'

'That's true. We'll give them a couple of minutes to get clear first.'

The two minutes of waiting seemed long. The rain was coming down steadily now, thick and straight.

Their clothes felt sodden when they stood up and their hair clung to their heads like rats' tails. But they scarcely noticed.

'OK, kids, then!' said Grandpa. 'Stay behind me. We have no intention of catching them up, right?'

They moved gingerly up the path in single file, with Claire bringing up the rear. There was no sign ahead of the three men. Jamie hoped they hadn't lost them by waiting too long.

Grandpa came to a halt. 'I want you two to stay here. We're coming to a lay-by that fishermen use to park their cars. I'm going to take a quick look round the corner.'

He tiptoed to the corner and took his quick look, then he disappeared round the other side. He was shielded from the children now by thick bushes.

'Claire, you stay where you are,' said Jamie. 'I'm just going to make sure Grandpa's all right.' After all, his grandmother had asked him to keep an eye on his grandfather. He went before Claire could object.

When he turned the corner he found Grandpa crouched in the bushes with his binoculars raised.

'Get down, Jamie!'

Jamie did as he was told. Grandpa had his glasses trained on a car parked a hundred metres or so further up the track. It was an old Land Rover with a steel roof rack. The three men were loading something – their catch, presumably – into the back. Then, when that was stowed away, they got into the car themselves.

'I can't make out the number plate. Dash it all!' said Grandpa. 'It's difficult with the rain. Here, Jamie, you have a go. Your eyes are younger than mine.'

Jamie took the glasses and put them to his eyes. Everything looked blurry. He twiddled the central piece to adjust the lenses. The car engine was starting up. He heard it humming. That was better! He could see the car now. It was beginning to move, to edge onto the track. He had the number plate in his sight but he couldn't read the number! He just couldn't. The rain was too heavy. He peered and he peered, following the car with the glasses. And then it had gone. Out of sight.

'That was the car I saw in the wood,' said Claire, who had been standing behind them, unnoticed.

'That's no help!' said Jamie. 'I didn't get the stupid number!'

Chapter Seven

'We could still go to the police,' said Jamie. 'And tell them what we saw.'

'We could,' agreed Grandpa. 'And we will. Once we've changed out of these clothes. We might get pneumonia if we don't and then your grandmother would have a few things to say!'

'But the men will get away,' cried Claire.

'There's no point in us rushing to a phone box. The police couldn't go chasing after every old Land Rover in the country!'

'I bet the man I saw in the wood was one of the poachers,' said Claire. 'He had the same kind of car.'

'He could have been,' agreed Jamie gloomily.

'What man was that, Claire?' asked Grandpa.

'Just someone I saw.'

'You didn't tell me about him.' Claire didn't answer. 'Did you?' pressed Grandpa.

'No.'

Grandpa humphed.

'I'm sorry.'

They headed back towards the river. At least the rain had stopped though there wasn't much sign of the sun coming out to dry them. It looked as if summer might be at an end.

They were due to go back to school next week anyway.

When they had gone part way down the track they heard a vehicle coming up behind them. They stopped and looked round.

'What if it's those men again!' Claire slipped her hand into her grandfather's.

This car was a Range Rover.

'It's Hector,' said Grandpa. 'And he's got Rory with him.'

The car drew up and the men greeted them.

'We got a tip off last night that poachers were in the area,' said Hector.

'We've been keeping watch right through the night,' said Rory, 'but we've had no luck.'

'We saw them!' said Claire.

'*You* did?' said Hector.

Grandpa told the men their story. 'But I'm afraid we didn't get the car number. Or a clear sighting of the men, either. It was raining cats and dogs the whole time.'

'I saw one of them in the wood earlier on,' said Claire. 'He had short black hair and he was wearing an anorak.'

'What colour anorak? Do you remember?' asked Rory.

Claire wasn't sure. She thought it might have been blue. 'Or a sort of grey.'

'Not an awful lot to go on,' sighed Hector. 'A lot of men have short dark hair.'

'Those poachers are bad news.' Rory shook his head. 'They'd empty the river of fish if they could get away with it.'

Another vehicle could now be heard approaching.

'This is getting to be like a motorway!' said Grandpa.

Who could it be this time?

'Grandma!' cried Jamie. 'It's Grandma!'

And indeed it was. She parked her car behind the Range Rover and got out.

'What on earth have you been doing?' she asked. 'Look at the three of you! Talk about drowned rats! Have you been *in* the river?'

'You weren't supposed to come for us till lunchtime,' said Grandpa.

'The rain woke me. When I saw how cold and wet it was I thought you might need something hot. I've brought a couple of flasks of hot chocolate and some fresh rolls.'

'Hot chocolate!' said Claire, who was beginning to shiver.

'By the looks of you I think I'm going to have to take you straight home and run a hot bath. You too, Jamie. And you, Grandpa!'

Grandma took time then to say hello to Hector and Rory. 'Seems like everybody's here this morning!'

'Grandma,' said Claire,' we've had an adventure.'

'An adventure?' Grandma didn't like the sound of that. 'What kind of adventure?'

They told her everything.

'But it didn't work out in the end,' said Claire sadly. 'They got away.'

'Seems they have,' said Hector. 'We're left with precious little to go on.'

'Oh, I don't know about that.' Grandma smiled. 'An old Land Rover, did you say, with a steel roof rack?'

'Have you seen one, Gran?' asked Jamie.

'I might have done.'

'Where, Margaret, where did you see it?' asked Grandpa.

'I went out sketching yesterday – you remember I said I would?'

'Yes, yes, go on!'

'And I came upon this clearing in the woods.'

'Was there an old Land Rover parked in it?' asked Claire.

'There was.'

'With a steel roof rack?' asked Jamie.

'With a steel roof rack.'

'And a man with short black hair?' asked Claire.

'There was no man there, not at that point, or I wouldn't have stayed. I did see a man later, though.'

'So what did you do?' asked Grandpa.

'I sat down and I drew some birds – you know I like drawing birds.

And then for fun I drew the Land Rover. I don't normally draw cars.'

'And, Margaret,' said Hector, 'did you by any chance put down the car's number?'

'Did you, Grandma?' cried Claire. 'Please say that you did!'

'As a matter of fact I did.'

'Brilliant!' cried Jamie.

'So where is it, your sketch book?' asked Grandpa.

'In the car.'

The children followed her to the car and waited while she rummaged inside for the book.

'Now where did I put it? It must be in here somewhere.'

'It must be!' cried Claire.

'I'm sure I didn't take it out,' said Grandma, frowning. There were quite a lot of things in the car. Tubes of paint, jars for holding water, even an easel. 'Ah, yes, here it is!' She took out the sketch book.

They crowded round while she rifled through the pages which were covered with animals and plants and birds. And there was the Land Rover, complete with roof rack *and* number plate!

Hector wrote the number quickly into his diary.

'That's the man!' cried Claire, pointing at the page.

At the side of the car Grandma had drawn a man with short dark hair. He had rather a long thin nose.

'He came back as I was packing up. I retreated into the bushes. He didn't see me.'

'That's wonderful, Margaret. I'm really grateful to you.' Hector took out his mobile phone. 'I'll ring the police straight away so that they can put out an alert for the men. They're bound to be heading south.'

After he'd made the call he and Rory jumped back into the Range Rover.

'We'll be in touch,' he promised. 'Just as soon as there's any news. Thanks!'

They drove off.

'Now,' said Grandma, 'I think you've all had enough adventures for one day. What do you say to coming home to a nice warm bath and a lovely hot breakfast of sizzling bacon and fresh eggs?'

Chapter Eight

They had their lovely hot breakfast and then Grandma suggested they might like to take a nap.

'You must be exhausted, the three of you. After all, you were up at the crack of dawn!'

They would never admit to being tired. How could they possibly *sleep*?

'We've got to wait and see if they catch the poachers,' said Jamie.

'They've *got* to catch them,' said

Claire fiercely. 'It won't be fair if they don't.'

The children went out into the garden and kicked a ball around. Every time they heard a car coming they raced to the gate. The local farmer went past, tooting his horn. And then the postman. They waved to both.

'Maybe they got away after all,' said Claire. 'The thieves. They might have driven really really fast. I expect thieves do.'

Jamie didn't answer. He didn't doubt that thieves would drive fast. But he was beginning to wonder if his grandmother might have written down the wrong number. It was possible. She was a bit short-sighted. Grandpa also thought that the poachers might have dirtied the number plate so that it couldn't be easily read. The number was all the police had to go on.

They couldn't stop every Land Rover in the country.

Jamie stood on a spar of the gate and hung over the top. Claire joined him. They watched the road. Another car came along but it was a blue saloon and they didn't know the driver. They waved to the driver, anyway.

Grandpa came out. He, too, was fidgety. 'No sign of Rory? Or Hector?'

Jamie shook his head. 'Nobody's phoned?'

'Not yet. But there's still time.'

'It's been *ages*,' groaned Claire.

Just then, they heard another car. They craned their necks as it turned the corner and came into sight. It was Rory in the Range Rover! They opened the gate and rushed to meet him.

'They got them!' shouted Rory. 'They got the men!'

The children cheered.

Rory got out of the car. He had a bag in his hand. 'They caught up with them about five miles this side of Glasgow. Another few minutes and they might well have disappeared inside some garage.'

'That's a relief!' said Grandpa.

Rory held up the bag. 'There's a fish in here for the detectives! From Hector. With his compliments.' He swung the bag over to Jamie, who took it.

'It's heavy,' he said.

'Look inside!' said Rory.

Jamie looked.

'What is it?' asked Claire.

'It's a salmon,' said Jamie. 'A big salmon!'

'That's handy,' said Grandma, who had joined them. 'I'd been wondering what to have for supper tonight.'

They thanked Rory and said goodbye. He drove off and they took the salmon into the kitchen. Grandma laid it out on a large platter.

'By the way, Margaret,' said Grandpa, 'how did you come to be in that particular clearing yesterday? Where the Land Rover was.'

'I was out sketching, wasn't I?'

'You weren't following us down the river by any chance?'

'Would I do that?'

'Yes!' cried the children. 'You would do that.'

Their grandmother smiled.

'Just as well you did, Grandma,' said Jamie. 'This time, at any rate.'

*Turn the page for more classic
Hodder Story Books....*

Another Hodder Children's Book

THE EGG THIEVES

Joan Lingard

It was Lecky Grant who saw the egg thieves leaving. Something wakened him early that morning. His house was opposite the pine wood where the ospreys had their nests.

Osprey eggs are very rare. People drive hundreds of miles to raid a nest. At one time the birds were wiped out altogether. Now Lecky's determined not to let it happen again: no egg thieves in his village!

h HODDER   Another Hodder Children's Book

TOM AND THE TREE HOUSE

Joan Lingard

Tom had always considered himself special. His parents had chosen him above anyone else. He was adopted.

But with the arrival of a new, real baby on the scene, Tom isn't so sure he's all that special any more. Maybe his parents didn't want him after all . . .

Retreating to his wonderful tree house, Tom looks for answers. But sometimes it's hardest to see what's right in front of your nose . . .

Another Hodder Children's Book

THE FAIRY COW

Ann Turnbull

"You've such a way with the cows, Megan," said Mrs Wynne the washerwoman, "it's a wonder the fairies don't take you to be their dairymaid."

Megan loves to tend her father's cows. And in her free time, she dreams of the lake over the hills. A magical place where magical creatures graze - the fairy cows.

Then Megan's father takes one captive. "She'll make our fortune," he says.

But the fairies are angry, and have their own special way of taking revenge . . .